Larry Burkett's
Great Smoky Mountains Storybook Series

Last Chance for Camp

Written by
Larry Burkett
with **K. Christie Bowler**

Illustrated by **Terry Julien**

MOODY PRESS
CHICAGO

Dedicated to
Anna Marie, Rebecca, Isah
and Isabella Sears & Jessica and Michael Phillips

Text & Illustrations ©1999 BURKETT & KIDS, LLC
Larry Burkett's Money Matters for Kids™
Executive Producer: *Allen Burkett*

For Lightwave
Managing Editor: *Elaine Osborne*
Art Director: *Terry Van Roon*
Desktop: *Andrew Jaster*

ISBN: 0-8024-0985-7
1 3 5 7 9 10 8 6 4 2
Printed in the United States of America

The Great Smoky Mountain Tales come to you from Larry Burkett's Money Matters for Kids™. In each tale, our family's children have fun while they learn how to best manage their money according to God's principles of stewardship.

This series of children's stories tells the adventures of the Carmichael family who live in a state park in the Great Smoky Mountains of North Carolina. The park is a beautiful setting, with a mist rising from the mountains like a smoky mist, giving them their name. Mom and Dad work in the park and, with their children Sarah, Joshua, and Carey, live in the rangers' compound not far inside the main park gate. Sarah, ten years old, is conscientious and loves doing things the right way. She has lots of energy, is artistic, and thinks before she acts. Her brother Joshua is eight and a half. Always doing something active, he's impulsive, adventurous, and eager to learn. Carey, their younger sister, is almost three and very cute. She loves doing whatever her sister and brother are doing. In the first four books of the series they learn how to save, how to give to the church, how to spend wisely, and how to earn money.

There's always something interesting going on in the Great Smoky Mountains, from hiking and horseback riding to fishing or panning for sapphires and rubies. Nearby, the town of Waynesville and, only a little farther away, the city of Asheville, provide all the family needs in the way of city amenities.

Through everyday adventures—from buying pet hamsters to dealing with the aftermath of a winter storm, from getting the right equipment in order to become an artist to going on summer camping trips—the children learn. Practical situations any child could face serve as the background for teaching about God's principles of stewardship.

Your children will love the stories and ask for more. Without even realizing it, they will, like our characters, learn in the middle of an adventure.

Mrs. Randall, the pastor's wife, quieted the children. Kids' Club was almost over and she had an announcement. When everyone was listening, she said, "We have a special surprise. This summer Kids' Club is going on a week long trip to Camp Daniel Boone!" She waited for the shouts to fade, then described what they would be doing. "We'll have crafts and Bible classes as usual. But Camp Daniel Boone also has horseback riding, canoeing, hiking, waterskiing, swimming, and team sports like baseball, volleyball, and basketball!"

The room broke out in cheers again. When it was quiet, she continued, "Anyone who wants to come must get permission from their parents and pay the registration fee of $40 by July 20th." She passed out papers with information about the camp.

Sarah looked at her brother. "Joshua, we just have to go. It will be great!"

"Yeah. Wait 'til Mom and Dad hear. They'll want us to go for sure." Sarah and Joshua's parents were Park Rangers in the Great Smoky Mountains State Park, and their love of the outdoors had rubbed off on their children.

When Sarah and Joshua were dropped off after Kids' Club, they raced into the house. "Guess what!" Joshua yelled. "Kids' Club is going to Camp Daniel Boone this summer."

"It's for a whole week and it costs hardly anything. Can we go? Please?" Sarah begged.

Dad took the paper from Sarah and read through it, then handed it to Mom. "What do you think?" he asked her.

"It looks like a wonderful trip," Mom said. "But it will cost you kids some money."

"I know," Sarah said. "The registration fees."

Josh nodded. "Then you'll pay the rest, right?" he asked with a grin. "It'll be good for us. You'll be glad we went because we'll learn all kinds of things."

Dad laughed. "You've convinced us. We'll pay for the camp if you two come up with your registration fees."

"Forty dollars is a lot for us," Sarah said. "Our allowance isn't near enough."

"True," Dad agreed. "But you can earn the rest. I'm sure we'll think of something."

A couple of days later Dad hung a white board in the family room. Written on it in big letters was "JOB BOARD." It was divided into four columns: "Job," "Description/ Qualifications," "Payment," and "Completed by."

Mom and Dad had listed a number of jobs on it, like "Wash and wax car." The description said, "Must be 6 years or older. Vacuum and dust inside of car. Close windows. Wash all outside parts with soap and water, including tires and hubcaps. Rinse thoroughly. Apply wax and shine." The payment was $5.00. Each job had a description like that. Some looked easy and wouldn't take long, but then they didn't pay as much as the harder ones.

"Now," said Mom, "you can do these jobs only after your regular chores."

"To take a job, write your name in the 'Completed by' column," Dad explained. "When you're done, Mom or I will inspect your work. You'll only be paid for jobs that we think are satisfactory. But if you do an excellent job, you could get a bonus. Understand?"

The kids nodded eagerly.

Sarah looked at the job board and sighed. Mom said these jobs came only after regular chores. She realized she had better clean her room. It wasn't her favorite chore, but she sure liked the results when she did it. And if she wanted to go to the camp she needed to earn some money.

She stood in her doorway and surveyed her room. "Hmm," she said. "Where to start?" She decided to begin with her clothes. Dirty ones went in the laundry basket, clean ones she folded and put back in the drawers. Then she organized her toys and books.

Meanwhile Joshua was playing with his friends Lee and Pedro.

"Are you going to Camp Daniel Boone?" Pedro asked. "I am!"

"You bet!" Lee said. "I've almost got my registration fee ready."

Joshua shrugged. "I don't. But I will. Maybe I should go and get a job off the board. See you guys tomorrow." He waved to his friends and returned home to look at the job board. Then he smiled, "I can tidy up the garage, no problem."

Joshua wrote his name on the board and headed to the garage. He was just beginning when Mom found him. "What are you up to?" she asked.

"I've taken this job off the board," Joshua said. "I know I can do it really well."

"I'm sure you can," Mom agreed. "Have you finished your regular chores?"

"Oops," Joshua gulped. "I forgot."

"You better clean up that room of yours, first," Mom said with a smile. "I'm sure you can do a really good job there, too."

Joshua sighed, wiped his name off the board, and headed upstairs. "Hmm. It's not all that bad," he thought, surprised. "This won't take long." He took a determined breath and got started.

Sarah looked around her room one more time. "Very nice," she said, nodding to herself. The room was neat and tidy. Her stuffed animal cuddled by her pillow, the floor and desk were clear. She smiled, went down to the job board, wrote her name by "Wash and wax car," and headed outside.

Joshua threw the clothes scattered around his room into the laundry basket. "Big improvement," he thought. Then he began picking up toys. When he found two changeable robots he'd thought were lost, he just couldn't help playing with them. They were so much fun he forgot all about cleaning his room.

Outside, Sarah enjoyed hearing the birds singing in the park trees all around their yard as she worked. She finished waxing the car. It looked shiny and clean in the afternoon sunshine—almost brand new. She rubbed the trunk one last time and went to get Dad.

With a very serious face, Dad walked all around the vehicle. He checked the wheels, fenders, and roof, and then looked inside. Sarah fidgeted. Did she do OK? She'd tried her best. Suddenly Dad grinned and shook her hand. "Excellent job, Miss Sarah. I think this deserves a bonus."

"Thanks!" Sarah said, eyes shining.

Dad laughed. "If you keep this up, you'll have your money in no time."

Sarah was so excited she ran right inside and took another job off the board.

On a beautiful, warm, sunny day two weeks later, Sarah and Joshua played basketball in their driveway. Sarah shot and scored. Joshua got the rebound and dribbled away, then back.

"I can hardly wait 'til camp," Sarah said, breathing hard. "I'm going to give my money to Mrs. Randall on Sunday. I'm even early."

Joshua shot and missed. "How come you got your money so fast?"

"I worked really hard," Sarah said. "I've done lots of jobs on the board. I even got bonuses for some! How about you?"

"Mm, not so good I guess," Joshua admitted. "I get distracted whenever I try to clean my room. But I have $12.50 already."

"That's not very much," Sarah told him doubtfully. "You've only got a week left to get your money."

"I'm not too worried," Joshua said. "I'm sure Dad will help me out. He really wants me to go to this camp."

Sunday, July 20th arrived. Joshua only had $19.00 for his registration. Sarah paid Mrs. Randall and then showed her receipt to Mom.

"Well done!" Mom gave her a hug. "What about you, Joshua? Will you pay yours today?"

"Uh, not exactly," Joshua mumbled. "I don't have enough."

"But today is the deadline," Mom said. "If you don't pay today, you can't go."

Suddenly it hit Joshua—he might actually miss camp because he'd been goofing off! Mrs. Randall said his Mom was right. But when she saw his disappointed face, she added, "Maybe we could save a place for you. But you must pay the registration fee the day before we leave. OK?"

"Thanks, Mrs. Randall. I will!" Joshua promised. Later he told Dad, "I've still got a chance. Can I borrow the money from you? I'll pay you back, I promise. There's no way I have time to earn it all now."

Dad sadly shook his head. "Sorry, Joshua. We had an agreement. And I don't want you to get into the habit of borrowing money instead of earning and saving it. It could get you in trouble."

Joshua almost cried. He really wanted to go to camp! But how could he ever get the money now?

Dad saw his sad face and said, "You made a mistake, Joshua, but it's not the end of the world. Do you understand where you went wrong?"

"I couldn't do jobs from the board because I kept getting behind in my regular chores."

"That's right. You were living in the present instead of thinking of the future. Then suddenly the future was here and you weren't ready for it."

"I thought there was lots of time, so I goofed off while Sarah worked. I won't do that again!"

Mom smiled. "There are still a couple of jobs on the board that would give you enough for the registration fee. They're hard ones, but if you're serious you can still do them."

"Really?" Joshua straightened up, his eyes bright.

"Sure. But it means working most of two weekends. Can you do that?" Dad asked.

Joshua nodded. If that was what it took to get to camp, he'd do it.

That weekend Joshua did his regular chores right away. Then he worked hard, cleaning the attic from end to end. He sorted and labeled boxes with all kinds of interesting things in them. He got distracted but remembered how much he wanted to go to camp and got back to work.

Joshua swept the floor and cleaned the walls. He got rid of the cobwebs, washed the windows, and hauled the garbage out to the curb. The boxes that were left he piled tidily against the wall, then painted the two short sidewalls light blue.

When he was done, Joshua stood in the middle of the attic and admired his work. It looked great! Why, this would make an awesome playroom! Mom and Dad came to inspect his work and gave Joshua a bonus for it. He grinned happily.

The next weekend Joshua worked hard again, this time with Dad. They repaired the fence, trimmed the trees and bushes, weeded the garden, and cut the grass. By the time they were done Joshua was exhausted. But he fell into bed that night knowing he had the money for camp.

The next day Joshua proudly paid Mrs. Randall his fee. That night he packed for camp, then fell into bed. He was still so tired he slept like a log. In fact, he slept right through his alarm. Mom shook him awake. "Come on, Joshua. You're almost late. You're going to camp today, remember?"

Suddenly Joshua was wide awake. "Oh no! Don't go without me." He quickly washed up, got dressed, and grabbed breakfast. Finally, he was ready. He dragged his pack out to the car where everyone was waiting. They got to church just as the bus was finished being loaded.

"Whew! Made it," Sarah breathed and carried her stuff to the bus. Soon they were waving good-bye.

The ride to Camp Daniel Boone was great! Everyone was excited and hyper. They sang songs, played games, and told jokes. Most of them had worked hard to get here. "You know," Joshua told Sarah, "it feels great knowing I did a good job, got a bonus, and paid my own way."

Sarah nodded. "Yeah. It makes camp even better. We earned it."

Camp Daniel Boone was fantastic! Joshua and Sarah went for an awesome overnight horseback trip. "Just like Daniel Boone used to do," Joshua thought, staring up at the stars. He'd never imagined there were so many! The counselors pointed out various constellations to the children. Out here you could see them all.

They went on a canoeing trip around the small lake. Lunch was fish they'd caught themselves, cooked over an open fire. It was the best fish they'd ever tasted.

They played sports, swam, played tricks and practical jokes, and had a fantastic time. Classes and Bible lessons were especially interesting, and the food was great.

Sarah and Joshua got to be good friends with the kids in their cabins. If anything went wrong, the counselors, who knew just how to make things wonderful, were right there to help.

The last night everyone sat around a big bonfire singing songs and telling what they'd learned at camp. It was a perfect way to end a great week.

The next morning all the kids piled back into the bus for the trip home. They were worn out from having so much fun, so it was a quieter trip this time.

Moms and dads were there to greet all the children when the bus pulled into the church parking lot. Sarah and Joshua said good-bye to their friends and ran over to Mom, Dad, and Carey to give them each a big hug. "Camp was the best!" they said together.

"And guess what!" Joshua added. "We're going to the amusement park in a couple of months. It has roller coasters and a Ferris wheel . . ."

"And a water ride and a pirate ship," Sarah added.

"Can you keep the job board going?" asked Joshua. "Then we can pay our own way again. But this time I'll work a little each weekend instead of leaving it all to the last minute!"

Dad laughed. "Sure! It helps us too, you know. Now what do you say to an ice cream on the way home?"

Earn Your Rewards!

"Work at everything you do with all your heart. Work as if you were working for the Lord, not for human masters" (Colossians 3:23 NIrV).

Work is good. If you do it right, you can accomplish all kinds of things and make life better for yourself and other people. The key is to develop a good attitude toward it when you're young.

Do the Four-Step

Learn to be a happy hard worker and you'll become a responsible, diligent, and trustworthy adult. You'll learn how to earn money and give value for value. How? By doing the "Diligence Four-Step."

1. Step 1: Work Hard. Do the job to the best of your ability. Organize yourself, get the tools out, and set to work. If you're sweeping the floor, get out the broom and dustpan, clear the floor so there's nothing in the way, then start at one end and move toward the other, getting all the spots.

2. Step 2: Work Well. Don't skip corners—literally. Don't sweep around objects. Make sure all of the dirt gets into the dustpan and then into the garbage, not under the mat. Do your best.

3. Step 3: Concentrate and Work Quickly. Don't put work off, thinking you'll do it later when you feel more like it. Get to work right away. Focus. Don't get distracted. Don't slow down thinking about something else or stop to chat with a friend. Do the best job you can in the least time possible.

4. Step 4: Do a Little Extra. Do more than you have to. Put the table and chairs back carefully, then dust them and wipe the counter. Do something you weren't asked to do.

Training Wanted!

Don't worry if you're not sure how to do a certain job yet. You can't be a good worker automatically. You need to learn, practice, and be trained. If you don't know how to do a job, or if it's your first time, ask for help from your parents or someone else who knows how to do that job. When they explain how to do it, listen carefully, ask questions to make sure you understand, then follow their directions. There are little things people learn that make jobs easier—"tricks of the trade." For example, there's a trick to getting all the dirt into the dustpan, making your bed quickly, mowing the lawn efficiently, and so on. When someone can show you the little tricks, work will be easier and faster.

When you learn the "Diligence Four-Step," you'll never lack for work. You'll get bonuses before other people and even get awards and promotions. That means you'll be given more responsibility and higher pay. People will trust you and want you to come to work for them because they'll know you'll do a good job. What a reward for a little training and a good attitude!

Larry Burkett's **Money Matters for Kids™** provides practical tips and tools children need to understand the biblical principles of stewardship. **Money Matters for Kids™** is committed to the next generation and is grounded in God's Word and living His principles. Its goal is *"Teaching Kids to Manage God's Gifts."*

Money Matters for Kids™ and **Money Matters for Teens™** materials are adapted by **Lightwave Publishing™** from the works of best selling author on business and personal finances, **Larry Burkett.** Larry is the founder and president of **Christian Financial Concepts™**, author of more than 50 books, and hosts a radio program "Money Matters" aired on more than 1,100 outlets worldwide. Money Matters for Kids™ has an entertaining and educational Web site for children, teens, and college students, along with a special **Financial Parenting™** Resource section for adults.

Visit Money Matters for Kids Web site at: **www.mm4kids.org**

building Christian faith in families

Lightwave Publishing is a recognized leader in developing quality resources that encourage, assist, and equip parents to build Christian faith in their families.

Lightwave Publishing also has a fun kids' Web site and an internet-based newsletter called *Tips & Tools for Spiritual Parenting.* This newsletter helps parents with issues such as answering their children's questions, helping make church more exciting, teaching children how to pray, and much more.

For more information, visit Lightwave's Web site: **www.lightwavepublishing.com**

MOODY
The Name You Can Trust
A MINISTRY OF MOODY BIBLE INSTITUTE

Moody Press, a ministry of Moody Bible Institute, is designed for education, evangelization, and edification.

If we may assist you in knowing more about Christ and the Christian life, please write us without obligation:
Moody Press, c/o MLM Chicago, Illinois 60610.
Or visit us at Moody's Web site: **www.moodypress.org**